2.85

Old M  h

D0886326

Published by The Trumpet Club, Inc., a subsidiary of Bantam Doubleday Dell Publishing Group, Inc.,
1540 Broadway, New York, New York 10036. "A Trumpet Club Special Edition" with the portrayal
of a trumpet and two circles is a registered trademark of Bantam Doubleday Dell Publishing Group, Inc

ISBN 0-440-83215-2 September 1994 UPR 10 9 8 7 6 5 4 3 2 1

OLD MOTHER WITCH

by
Carol Carrick

Pictures by
Donald Carrick

A TRUMPET CLUB SPECIAL EDITION

David's doorbell rang.

"Get the candy! Get the candy!" David yelled to his mother. "They're starting to come."

He opened the door.

"Trick or treat," shouted the tramp standing there.

David laughed. It was Scottie. They were going out together this Halloween night.

"Are you ready?"

"Sure. Let's go!"

"Don't trip over your tail, kitty," David's mother called as they ran down the walk.

They passed Mrs. Oliver's house next door. David hated Mrs. Oliver. She was a real old crank. The kids called her "Old Mother Witch." She complained if they roller skated in front of her house and she even chased the dogs out of her yard.

One time David's mother had sent him over with flowers from their garden but Old Mother Witch wouldn't answer the door. If David hit his ball too hard and it went over the fence, she scolded him when he went in her yard to get it. Mary Ellen said she knew it was Old Mother Witch who had poisoned her cat because it had hung around her birdbath.

"This is what Oliver looks like." David drew a picture of an old hag on the sidewalk with his chunk of Halloween chalk.

"Hey, that's great! Put a wart on the end of her nose," said Scott.

David added the wart. Then he wrote in big letters, OLD MOTHER WITCH, and drew an arrow pointing toward Mrs. Oliver's house.

Scott gave David a shove through the gate. "Ring Oliver's bell."

"Hey! Not me!" yelled David. They started scuffling and shoving each other.

"Come on. Let's go to the Bridwells'," Scott said.

There was a big jack-o'-lantern on the Bridwells' porch and their front door was ajar. When David and Scott got up on the porch they heard a terrible cackle.

"Come in, sonny. Why don't any of you little boys want my candy?" And a witch popped her head out the door.

The boys knew it was Mrs. Bridwell in a witch's costume. Even so, they felt a little uneasy when they had to get close enough for her to put some candy into their sacks.

Mary Ellen and Eric were coming up the walk.

"Trick or treat!"

"Come with us," Mary Ellen said. "We're going over to the next block."

They went to every house where a porch light was on
to welcome them. Between these bright stretches,
shadowy figures popped out at them from behind
bushes. Small white ghosts fluttered on front lawns. The
streets echoed with the clatter of running feet and the
screams of excited children.

Then their bags grew heavy. They felt cold and tired
and it really wasn't much fun any more.

"Let's go to my house," said David. "My mom said
she'd make us some hot chocolate with marshmallows."

As they passed the dark house next to David's, Mary Ellen said, "Old Mother Witch isn't home. Maybe she's out on her broomstick."

"No, she's just sitting in the dark so no one will ring her bell," said David.

"Hey, let's do it anyway," whispered Eric, pinching David's arm with excitement. "And if she doesn't answer the door we'll play a trick on her."

"Naahh," answered David. "Let's just go to my house."

"You're afraid of that old lady."

"No, I'm not," David said. "I just don't feel like it."

"Oh sure," sneered Eric. "I know what kind of cat you are. You're a scairdy cat." And he pulled on David's tail.

"Yeah. Let's see you ring her bell, scairdy cat," Scott joined in, pushing David toward the gate as he had before.

"Cut it out!"

"Here kitty, kitty," Mary Ellen called.

And then they all started calling "kitty" and meowing.

"All right. All right. Shut up! She'll hear you."

Before David could stop and think about how scared he really was, he had opened the gate and was sneaking up the path to the front door. He could feel Old Mother Witch watching from one of the dark windows.

He tiptoed slowly and carefully up the creaking steps to the porch. He could see nothing at all but a gleam from the streetlight on the glass of the front door. He could hear the others giggle nervously behind the bushes.

Suddenly the wind blew the screen door open and it banged against the house. David froze. There were rustling sounds. Then he saw papers and garbage blowing off the porch.

He made a dash for the front door, tripped over something, and fell against an overturned garbage can. It rolled noisily to the other end of the porch.

"Oh boy," muttered David. "Now I'm really in for it. She must have heard that."

As he scrambled to his feet his hand reached out. What he had tripped over was something soft. He screamed and heard the others scream and run down the block. He had touched skin and a pair of eyeglasses. It was a body. It was Mrs. Oliver.

"She's dead!" David yelled.

He quickly pulled away from the body. He had never touched a dead person before. Then he leaned forward and tried to see her in the darkness.

"Mrs. Oliver," he called timidly.

He heard a coarse whisper.

"Help me."

David jerked away again and waited. She didn't move. Maybe she really hadn't said anything either. He looked around. Down the block the other kids were huddled under the street light looking toward him. He could see his own comforting porch light next door.

He didn't remember running home or yelling, "Mom!"

But he felt the warmth from the house as his mother opened their front door. How solid she seemed as he held her around the waist. Her sweater was soft against his face.

"Why, David! What's the matter?"

"Mrs. Oliver is dead! She's lying on her porch and she's dead!"

"Go see what it is," she said to his father. "I'll call the police."

His mother stroked David's hair after she dialed the emergency number. And when she was through with the call she sat down with him and said, "Now tell me what happened."

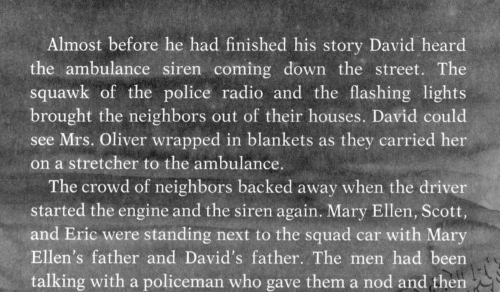

Almost before he had finished his story David heard the ambulance siren coming down the street. The squawk of the police radio and the flashing lights brought the neighbors out of their houses. David could see Mrs. Oliver wrapped in blankets as they carried her on a stretcher to the ambulance.

The crowd of neighbors backed away when the driver started the engine and the siren again. Mary Ellen, Scott, and Eric were standing next to the squad car with Mary Ellen's father and David's father. The men had been talking with a policeman who gave them a nod and then walked up to David's house.

In all the excitement David had forgotten he was still wearing the pussycat costume. All that Halloween scary stuff seemed silly now that something really frightening had happened.

"Is this the boy who found Mrs. Oliver?" The policeman asked David's mother.

David felt as though he had done something wrong, but the policeman only wanted to know how he had found her and in what position she had been lying.

"Is she dead?" asked David.

"Not if they get her to the hospital in time," the policeman said. "She must have been taking out the trash after she thought all you kids had gone home. The ambulance attendant thinks she had a heart attack. You may have saved her life."

That night when David went to bed he missed the light that usually shone on his wall from the house next door. He thought about how scared he was when he found Mrs. Oliver. Then he thought about how scared she must have been, too, lying on the porch unable to get help. He felt sorry that they had been trying to bother her. It was almost as though they had made her sick.

On the way to the school the next day, David was ashamed to see the witch he had drawn on the sidewalk. He tried to scuff away the ugly picture and the words OLD MOTHER WITCH with the sole of his sneaker. Witches were mean and powerful. Mrs. Oliver was just an old lady. Maybe she wasn't even coming back.

Someone had left the gate open and two dogs were sniffing around the spilled garbage. David chased them off and picked up as much of the mess as he could. He ran to school feeling a little better.

For weeks there was still no light on in the house next door. But just before Thanksgiving David's mother told him Mrs. Oliver had come home in a taxi.

Every day now a visiting homemaker came to help her. David tried to catch a peek of Mrs. Oliver when she answered the door to see if she looked different. But he never did see her.

Then one morning David saw Mrs. Oliver coming up to his front door. Maybe she was going to complain to his mother about Halloween night.

He waited for her knock but he didn't want to go to the door. Since he had been able to do something for her, he felt better about her. But he still didn't want to speak to her. He wouldn't know what to say.

Maybe she changed her mind and felt too shy to speak to them, too, because David saw her turn from the door and hurry away. At least, she hurried as fast as an old woman who is leaning on a cane *can* hurry.

When David had to leave for school, he found a bag hanging on the knob of the front door. Inside there were chocolate chip cookies and a note that only said, *Thank You.*

But David knew who it was from.